This book belongs to

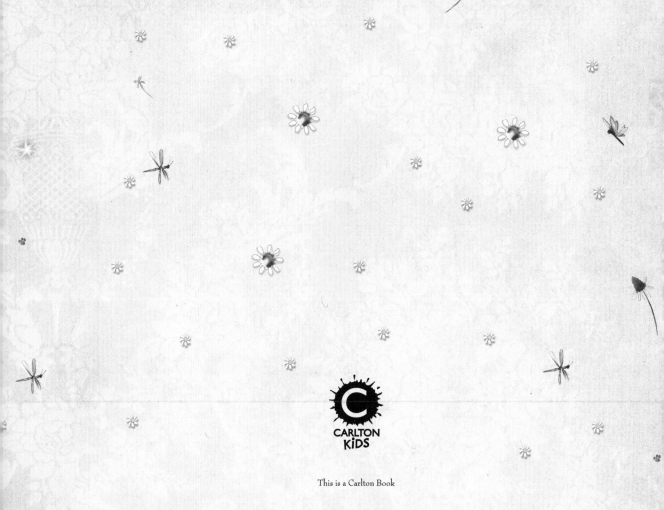

This is a Carlton Book

Published in 2016 by Carlton Books Ltd,
an imprint of the Carlton Publishing Group,
20 Mortimer Street, London W1T 3JW

Design copyright © 2016 Carlton Books Ltd
Text copyright © 2007 Caitlin Matthews
Illustrations © Bee Willey 2007

ISBN: 978-1-78312-218-9

Printed in China

Executive Editor: Bryony Davies
Editor: Anna Brett
Creative Director: Clare Baggaley
Designer: Alison Tutton

The Perfectly Royal
PRINCESS
Handbook

CAITLIN MATTHEWS

ILLUSTRATED BY BEE WILLEY

CONTENTS

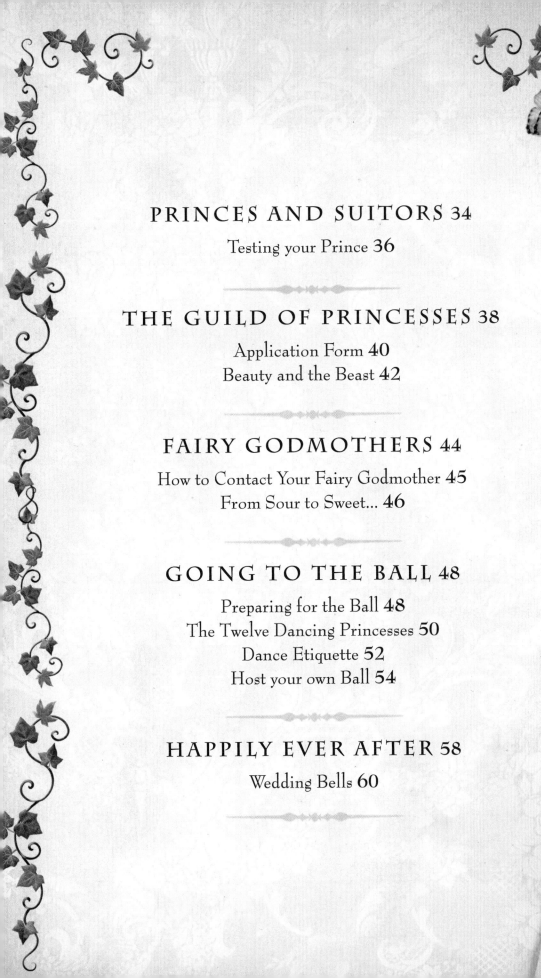

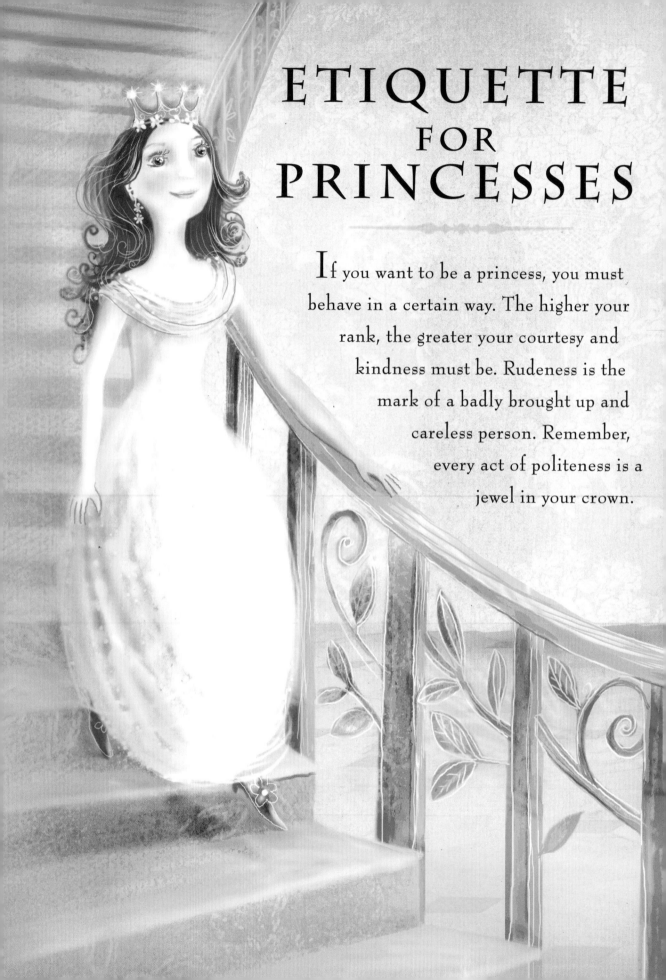

ETIQUETTE
FOR
PRINCESSES

If you want to be a princess, you must behave in a certain way. The higher your rank, the greater your courtesy and kindness must be. Rudeness is the mark of a badly brought up and careless person. Remember, every act of politeness is a jewel in your crown.

The first thing every princess should do is live their life according to Princess Ariadne's rules – she is the founder of the Guild of Princesses.

* *Be polite to enemies*
* *Be considerate to equals*
* *Respect your elders*
* *Be kind to subjects and servants*
* *Be courteous to strangers*

A 'REAL' PRINCESS

You can always tell a real princess by the way she behaves: she has good manners, excellent deportment (that's the way you walk, stand and sit) and a certain delicacy. My friend Princess Helena is a good example of exquisite breeding; she was able to feel a pea through 20 mattresses – only a real princess could do that! You can read her story over the page…

The Princess
and the Pea

There was once a very handsome prince who was determined to marry a true princess. He'd had problems before with ladies who said they were princesses but turned out not to be, and some princesses who weren't quite as well-bred and delicate as he'd expected. He sent out a proclamation saying, "Prince Adrian seeks a wife: only real princesses need apply."

Princesses came to his castle by the carriage-load. First Prince Adrian received them in the hall with his parents, where they spoke to each lady. If Prince Adrian liked one, he would ask his mother, the queen, to lead her to a bed-chamber to stay the night. In the morning, it was soon clear who was a well-bred princess and who was not.

When it seemed as if no lady was good enough to be his wife, one evening Princess Helena knocked on the castle door and asked to meet the prince. Prince Adrian liked the look of her: she was polite and elegant, as well as intelligent. So he sent her to his mother who led Helena to the bed-chamber she had prepared.

The queen had put one little, hard pea on the wooden bed and then ordered that 20 mattresses be laid on top of it. This was her secret test for every princess. Helena had to climb a very long ladder to get into this extraordinary bed. In the morning, the queen brought her breakfast and asked how she had slept. "I'm afraid I didn't sleep much at all. There was something poking into my back," said Helena, reluctantly, because she didn't want to offend the queen.

The queen smiled and rushed to her son. "We have found your future wife! She didn't sleep a single wink because of the little pea poking into her back. She felt it through all the mattresses – something none of the other ladies could feel!"

PRINCESSLY POLITENESS

As a princess, you should:

❀ Be polite to everyone, whether they are a prince, a ploughman, a duchess or a servant.

❀ Be kind and considerate. If your lady in waiting has been up all night sewing 568 pearls onto your new ball dress, remember to thank her and don't ask her to supervise the seating plan at the banquet the next morning as well.

❀ Be respectful. Greet and bid farewell to everyone graciously; notice who is present.

❀ Be grateful. Thank people for gifts or services in person or by letter. Don't take them for granted.

❀ Be honourable. Be on time for your appointments and don't forget to keep your promises.

❀ Be true to your friends and don't gossip about them or tell any secrets that they've trusted you with.

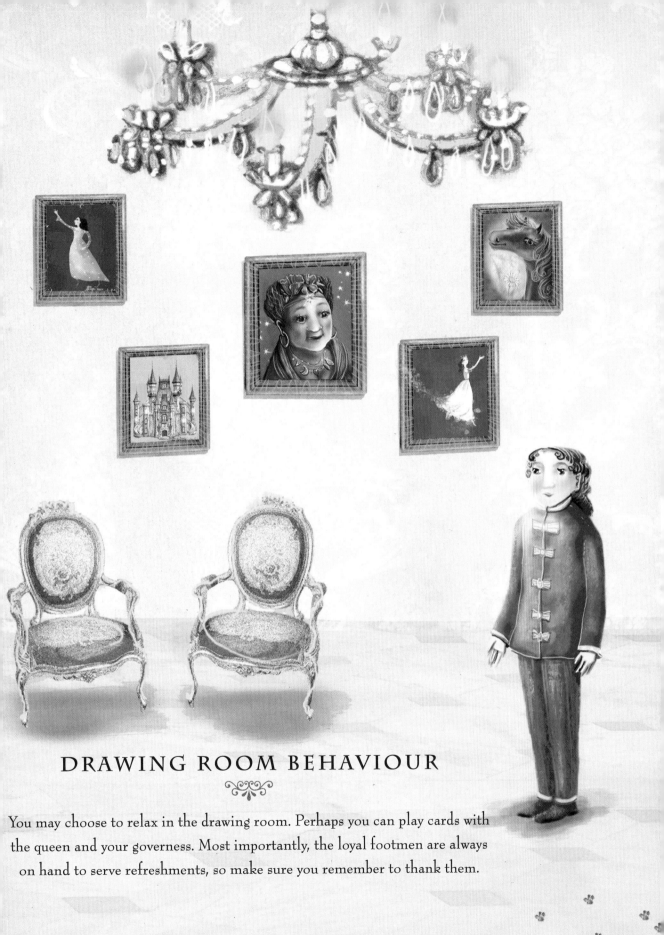

DRAWING ROOM BEHAVIOUR

You may choose to relax in the drawing room. Perhaps you can play cards with the queen and your governess. Most importantly, the loyal footmen are always on hand to serve refreshments, so make sure you remember to thank them.

DEPORTMENT

MOVE LIKE A PRINCESS

A princess needs to learn how to walk and move in an elegant way. First of all, you should learn how to walk in a long skirt. If you don't have a long skirt, fetch a shawl or towel and tie it around your waist with a piece of string or a scarf.

First, slide your right foot gently forward and take a step, then bring your left foot forward in the same way. Practise walking slowly in a straight line, then try walking in a circle.

If you have a long mirror, walk in front of it. If it looks like you're wading through a river in boots, then you're probably not going to be the most elegant princess! Try walking from your knees down rather than from your thighs and hips: this keeps your body still and makes you take small, delicate steps.

WALKING UP AND DOWN STAIRS

The trick to going up stairs is to bend your knees before the first step, and with one hand elegantly pick up a fold of your skirt so that it doesn't get caught. When you reach the top, allow the fold to drop. When walking down stairs, keep one hand lightly on the banister while using the other to slightly lift the back of your skirt, allowing it to fall when you reach the ground level.

SITTING

When you sit down, keep your back straight. Don't cross your legs or raise your feet above your hips. And don't fidget!

From Princess to Goosegirl and Back Again

A TRUE STORY BY PRINCESS PETAL

I was born Princess Petal of Mittelburg. When Father died my mother arranged for me to marry a prince that I had never met, from far away. Preparing for my journey to meet the prince, she packed my jewels away into a bag. Then, cutting her finger with a sharp knife and letting three bright drops of blood fall upon her handkerchief, she said, "Dear Petal, keep this handkerchief with you always. It will advise you when I'm not with you!"

I rode away on my horse, Fallada, with only my maid Pertal as company. As we rode I became thirsty so I dismounted and stretched out my hand into the river for a drink. My mother's handkerchief fell into the water. Suddenly, all my strength left me and I fainted. When I awoke, Pertal had stolen my clothes, my jewels and taken my horse, leaving me to follow on foot with only her maid's clothes to wear.

Bells were ringing in celebration when I arrived at the castle. I asked the people what had happened and they replied, "Don't you know that Princess Petal has just married Prince Pallas?"

Pertal had stolen my name! Pretending to be me, she had married my future husband! I sat down on the bottom step of the tower and wept. To survive I became a goosegirl.

Pertal was so worried that Prince Pallas would find out that she was not Princess Petal that she had poor, dear Fallada, my faithful horse, killed. To make my life even more miserable, she ordered that Fallada's head be displayed over the gate through which I drove the geese into the meadow each day. Every morning I said to him, "Poor Fallada, hanging there!" And Fallada's head would say quietly back to me:

Poor Princess in despair
If your mother only knew
Her heart would break in two!

Every day was the same as the last, but I didn't realize that Conrad, a gooseboy I worked with, had heard Fallada speaking to me. He told the king that I spoke to the horse's head each day and that Fallada always replied. The king's eyes opened wide when he heard this. He knew something was wrong: his son wasn't happy with his new wife, who was a lady without any manners at all.

That night, the king asked me to tell him the truth. I replied that I'd sworn not to tell a living thing. Leaving the room he said, "Well if you can't tell any living thing, why don't you tell the truth to this iron stove here?" And so I knelt down before the stove and poured out the whole story, sobbing until my heart would break.

What I didn't know was that the kind old king was just outside, listening to everything. He told Prince Pallas, who was very relieved to hear that his wife was in fact a maid because he didn't like her at all.

At a great banquet that night, the old king asked Pertal a riddle: "What would you do to a maid who disobeyed her mistress, stole her jewels, pretended to be her mistress and then married her husband to be?"

Pertal replied, "She would deserve to be stripped to her petticoat and pecked out of town by geese."

"Wicked girl!" said the king, "You are that maid and shall suffer your own judgment!"

So Pertal was stripped to her petticoat and the geese, who were really quite fond of me, pecked and pecked her till her petticoat was full of holes. She ran out of town, never to be seen again.

I was finally married to Prince Pallas and we have lived together happily ever since. He privately calls me Lady Goosegirl, although I am always known as Her Serene Highness Princess Petal on state occasions.

THE BEAUTY OF A PRINCESS

Every princess is naturally beautiful. The secret of true beauty is to be content with yourself. This means not being ashamed of your looks or believing people who tell you unkind things. Make the most of your best features: ask a good friend to tell you what these are. Here are some tips and tricks to help your natural beauty shine through.

BEAUTY AT HOME

Beauty begins in the bathroom.
Cleanliness is the mark of a noble person.
Wash your face, hair and body regularly.
A dirty princess in a beautiful dress still
looks like a dirty princess! To keep your
skin looking fresh, don't eat too many
sweets or cakes, and be sure to take plenty
of exercise and wear the clothes and
colours that suit you.

PRINCESS RAPUNZEL'S GUIDE TO BEAUTIFUL HAIR

The crowning glory of a princess is her hair. My tresses are the longest in the Guild of Princesses. To keep your hair beautiful, wash and comb it regularly. Brush your hair with 100 strokes before bed and it could become as beautiful as mine!

PRINCESS CORDELIA'S GUIDE TO DRESSING

One of the greatest advantages of being a princess is the clothes and jewels. You will have to wear a great variety of clothes on many different occasions. People expect you to be in a new gown for very special events like balls, so do remember to pass your old dresses down to your ladies in waiting. Here's a guide to some of the outfits you'll need to carry out your duties:

RECEPTIONS AND FOREIGN VISITS

These are occasions to shine, so take a selection of beautiful dresses. Wear your richest jewels so that everyone can see you at your best.

INSPECTING THE GUARD

Wear a neat hat with a cockade, an elegant jacket, a long woollen skirt and buttoned boots. If you are going to inspect the troops on horseback, then you will need a special riding dress for riding side saddle.

TRAVELLING ABOUT THE KINGDOM

A coloured dress and cloak with simple jewels is best for these occasions. When you need to see how things really are in your kingdom, choose the clothes of a gentlewoman – a plain but well-made dress, a cloak of dark colours and a little hat with a fine veil so that people don't know who you are.

BALLS AND BANQUETS

For these events you will need long gloves, an off-the-shoulder pale ball gown with a gauze overskirt and delicate dancing shoes. Wear your tiara or coronet over a splendid hairstyle, and one very beautiful necklace.

PRIZE-GIVING AT FARM SHOWS

These occasions can often be very muddy so long boots are essential, and because you will want to pat a lot of animals I suggest some warm leather gloves. You can still look elegant with a hat and a colourful, warm jacket.

VISITING HOSPITALS

Sick people get very tired of seeing the same things every day, so wear something pretty and colourful to cheer them up. Carry a bunch of flowers or herbs and give everyone you visit a little sprig.

ROYAL DUTIES

What does a princess do all day? I expect you think we have lots of free time and are able to eat unlimited chocolates? Wrong! Being a princess means you have to serve your people and be available to them for many hours every day. Although you may have prettier clothes and richer jewels than anyone else, you can't just do what you want.

For instance, at state banquets everyone is placed according to their rank or importance. It's quite possible that you will be sitting next to a very dull general or a boring minister more often than you will be next to a handsome prince or a female friend. The secret is to listen to your guests as if what they are saying is the most interesting thing in the world.

TIPS FOR ROYAL DUTIES

Here are a few tips to help you get through the day:

❀ Smile and be gracious, even when you may not feel like it.

❀ When greeting guests, make them feel comfortable and at ease. The secret of this is to think of your guest's needs first.

❀ Not everyone can meet you personally; remember to wave graciously to the crowds as if they were all known to you.

❀ Wear a pair of silk or soft leather gloves: you might have to shake hands with up to 100 people at an event!

❀ If you need to stifle a yawn, press the tip of your tongue to the roof of your mouth, suck in your cheeks, and breathe deeply in and out.

WEARING YOUR CROWN

People like to see you wearing your crown, but it can be very heavy. For everyday duties I personally prefer a little tiara, which is much lighter. Some princesses were made to walk with books balanced on the top of their heads when they were girls to help prepare them for crown-wearing.

HOW TO CURTSY

A curtsy is a respectful bow to someone that you're meeting. Stand up and transfer your weight to your left foot. Now position your right foot behind your left heel, and set your right toe down as you slowly sink down, bending both knees. The trick is to smoothly move down while keeping your body upright, and incline your head a little. Now look up charmingly and smile, extending one hand for the person you're curtsying to, to take or kiss.

A DAY IN THE LIFE
OF A PRINCESS

6.45am:
Rise, wash, dress and check
the day's schedule. Dictate
letters of thanks.

8am:
Breakfast with the
royal family.

9.30am:
Presentation of medals to the heroes
of the Loyal Regiment.

11.30am:
Cutting the ribbon on
the new town fountain
and declaring it open.

12.30pm:
Lunch at the Ladies' Guild.

4pm:
Riding lesson.

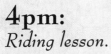

5.30pm:
Sewing circle of Guild of Princesses and packing parcels for orphans' birthdays.

6.30pm:
Bath and change.

7.30pm:
Dinner with the Ambassador of Arbery.

9.30pm:
Retire and bed.

Fair Vasilissa the Wise Princess

Vasilissa lived with her stepmother and stepsisters. One dark winter
night, the fire went out and her stepmother cruelly sent Vasilissa
out in a snowstorm to fetch more wood. Vasilissa wrapped her shawl
around her and, with only the doll that her mother had given her in
her pocket, ran through the forest. The doll guided her to a clearing
where she found a house on chicken legs, surrounded by a fence of
skulls on poles. This was the house of the witch, Baba Yaga.

Vasilissa was very frightened, but the witch asked,
"Did you come here of your free will, or were you sent?"
"I was sent," replied Vasilissa.
"Then be my faithful servant and you will have your desire,"
said the witch.

For many days and nights Vasilissa served Baba Yaga who set her
difficult tasks, such as sorting sacks of mixed seeds into separate
piles, but Vasilissa was always guided by her mother's doll, who
gave her wise help. Now, only Baba Yaga could open the front door,

but the chicken-legged house had never been so clean and as a reward, while Vasilissa polished the door, it opened by itself. She ran outside, picked up one of the skull-lanterns and raced home through the forest.

At the sight of the glowing-eyed light, the stepmother and her daughters fled in fear. Now she was alone, Vasilissa walked into town and found lodgings with an old woman. Here she began making beautiful linen shirts. The old woman took these to the Tsar's son, pretending they were her own work.

The Tsarevitch liked the shirts so much that he demanded more and more, so many that the old woman was forced to admit that they were not her own work after all. Finally, the prince met Vasilissa and fell in love with her. To this day, fair Vasilissa still listens to the doll in her pocket, and everyone thinks her the wisest princess in the world.

A REALM OF
YOUR OWN

Ruling your realm fairly and with compassion means that you need to know your land and its people well. You also have to be neighbourly to the countries that adjoin yours, otherwise you could end up with enemies. Be a wise and loving ruler by following these guidelines.

GETTING TO KNOW
YOUR REALM

Go to a high place and look over your realm on a sunny day, so that you can learn to love it even better. See the people at work, the animals in the fields, the trees, the flowing rivers, and then remember that one day, when you become queen, they will all depend on your wise rule.

TIPS FOR RULING YOUR REALM

- Make alliances and friends wherever you go. A smile costs nothing!

- Watch your enemies and rivals. Many a princess has come to grief by not keeping her enemies nearby. You may not like them, but if you can see them at least you have some idea of what they're planning!

- Don't make enemies by promoting your family and friends above everyone else.

- Don't tolerate cruelty to animals. When in trouble, many in the Guild of Princesses have had their lives saved by animals to whom they showed kindness.

- Don't listen to gossip. The court is a small place. Rumours and stories circulate quickly and often come to nothing.

- Be resourceful. You never know when circumstances will change. A princess today, or an outcast tomorrow? Cultivate skills that will help you survive in the real world: a little light embroidery today may help you hem your landlady's sheets tomorrow. Kingdoms come and kingdoms go, so be prepared!

THINGS PRINCESSES SHOULD AVOID

Many people are jealous of princesses. They send them gifts that turn out to be traps, like a truth cloak that shrinks when it's worn by a liar! Also beware of:

• The water horse, which appears to be an ordinary horse until it dives into deep water while its rider is still mounted.

• Presents of gloves with sharp needles hidden in them.

• Any unknown potions, drinks and apples that might be poisoned.

• Gifts of basilisk eggs for the palace zoo (a basilisk is a serpent that is so deadly even its breath could harm you). When a basilisk hatches, it can turn you to stone.

The Knights' Princess

Long ago, in Olveria, there was an old king with three daughters. One day, his daughters Carolina, Assuntina and Fanta-Ghirò found him sitting with his head in his hands, for the land of Arbery had declared war upon them.

Because the king was unwell, each daughter in turn offered to lead the army as a general. The king replied, "It's no task for a woman. If I find you thinking like a woman, I'll have you sent home!"

Carolina and Assuntina went out with the army, but they were distracted by the soldiers' clothes and by the glorious fruits upon the trees. They were both sent home.

So, beautiful Fanta-Ghirò dressed herself in knightly armour and went out to meet the enemy. Prince Lorenzo led the opposing army; he suspected the general might be a woman so he invited her home and asked his mother to set tests to see if she was a man or a woman.

The queen told Lorenzo to take Fanta-Ghirò to inspect the weapons.
She talked enthusiastically about pistols and swords, just like a man.
Then Lorenzo took the general to the garden where Fanta-Ghirò broke
off a sprig of jasmine and stuck it behind her ear, just like a man. Then
the queen suggested a final test: Fanta-Ghirò should dive into the pool.
Lorenzo stripped off his shirt and plunged in.

Just as Fanta-Ghirò was about to take off her clothes, an urgent letter
arrived saying her father's health was much worse. Leaving a note for
Lorenzo to find, she rode home.

A woman came, a woman went home,
And the king never guessed who threatened his throne.

Lorenzo knew for certain then and rode to Olveria to ask for the
general's hand in marriage. From that day to this there was peace between
Olveria and Arbery – all due to Fanta-Ghirò's wit and beauty!

PRINCES and SUITORS

When you're a princess, the time will come when you need to get married. Of course, not all suitors will be to your liking. Princesses have always had to be very clever in order to avoid marrying princes they don't like. Sometimes the available princes are very boring and stuffy, sometimes they aren't handsome enough and sometimes they are just plain cruel. The best thing is to test them first and check that they're worthy of marriage!

TESTING YOUR PRINCE

Here at the editorial office of *Precious Princess* (the only magazine just for princesses) we receive many letters about choosing the right prince. Some look handsome but turn out to be very stupid. Some pretend to love you, but actually don't care at all. To live 'happily ever after' you must make good choices about suitors. So how can you tell? We've come up with these key questions to help you test your prince.

1. Which of these does your potential prince smell of?

a) Cheese
b) Sweat and body odour
c) Fresh water and nature

2. Your prince thinks Shakespeare is:

a) Your neighbour's cat
b) A tiny village
c) A poet and playwright

3. Where does the man in question spend most of his time?

a) In front of the mirror
b) With his mummy
c) Riding his horse

4. When you look at his face, what is the most obvious feature?

a) His monobrow
b) His large nose
c) His bright blue eyes

5. Your prince's best friend is:

a) His goldfish
b) His sister
c) The champion knight

6. Your friend falls over in the mud when out walking. How does your potential partner react?

a) Points and laughs
b) Keeps on walking
c) Helps her up and offers her his jacket

7. Your prince produces a gift to try and woo you. Is it:

a) A new broom for the stables?
b) A trip for two to the next jousting tournament?
c) Flowers in your favourite colour?

———◆◆◆———

Answers

Mostly As – Avoid! *This man is a silly, smelly, ugly, unromantic loner who definitely doesn't deserve you!*

Mostly Bs – Brush him off! *He has potential but you can do much better.*

**Mostly Cs – He's your Prince Charming! You're a match made in heaven.*

THE GUILD OF PRINCESSES

All princesses belong to the Guild of Princesses (GOP), which was founded by Princess Ariadne many centuries ago. She was abandoned by Prince Theseus and has since dedicated her life to the support of all princesses. Princess Ariadne continues to guide the Guild with the help of long-term members. We all support each other, do many good deeds, such as helping at the School for Wayward Princesses, and meet often, especially to welcome new members as we are doing today.

Ever Royal *Semper Regalem* *Semper Pulchram* *Ever Beautiful*

APPLICATION FORM

Answer all the questions on this form to be considered for membership.

1. You see a magical tree crying "shake me, shake me". Do you:

a) Ignore it?

b) Pick one apple?

c) Shake the tree?

2. You are unjustly cast out of your home. Do you:

a) Sit down and cry?

b) Write a letter of complaint?

c) Hire yourself out as a servant?

3. Your suitor has become a frog. Do you:

a) Look for another suitor?

b) Make him a nice pond?

c) Kiss him?

4. Your father marries again and your stepmother and her children are unkind to you. Do you:

a) Sulk?

b) Put beetles in their soup?

c) Respect your father's choice and try to be pleasant to them?

5. You are forbidden to attend the ball. Do you:

a) Stamp your foot?

b) Sneak in through the kitchen?

c) Call on your Fairy Godmother for help?

6. You meet a stranger on the road who offers you a piece of fruit. Do you:

a) Eat it?

b) Ask where it came from?

c) Politely decline?

7. Your father is about to marry you to a man you hate. Do you:

a) Put up with your husband?

b) Try to enjoy the pretty clothes he buys you?

c) Run away?

Answers How did you do in your application to join the Guild of Princesses? If you chose: a) You receive no points at all. b) Give yourself 1 point for trying. c) Give yourself 3 points for being wise.

Total your score and reveal your result: 18–21 points: You come highly recommended. Join our queens in waiting! 12–18 points: You are definitely princess material! Well done! 5–12 points: You are a survivor and show some promise, but you need to be more considerate. Read this book again and see if you can learn something! 0–5 points: Sorry, you don't fit our exacting standards. Apply again later when you've learned a little more about being a princess.

GUILD OF PRINCESSES RULES

- All princesses **must be approved by** the inner circle of GOP.
- Princesses must be **elegant, beautiful and gracious** at all times.
- Members of **ten years** or over are expected to lead princess classes once a year.
- Princesses must attend at least **four GOP meetings a year** and may apply to host the annual Princess Reunion once every seven years.
- Members must **contribute to the welfare fund** for the School for Wayward Princesses.
- Princesses must **offer hospitality** to other GOP members when they travel.
- Members must spend at least a week every year working in the **Retired Princesses Home**.
- Those who lapse from our high standards will receive **three solemn warnings** before their membership and privileges are **cancelled**.

PRIVILEGES

In return for your membership, you are given the following privileges:

- In the event of the loss of your realm, we will look after you.
- We provide a holiday resort for you to rest from your duties.
- Your portrait will be painted and hung in the corridor of honour at our castle headquarters.
- You will be featured in Precious Princess, the GOP magazine.
- On your birthday the GOP will host a special party for you, when you will receive a surprise birthday present.
- You have the right to display the GOP insignia on your carriage for our efficient Fairy Godmother Breakdown Service – carriages and horses will be retrieved from all parts of the world!

Beauty and the Beast

Once upon a time, there lived a merchant who promised to bring back gifts to his three daughters when he returned from a long voyage. On his way home, he realized that he had forgotten to bring something for Bellinda, his youngest daughter. As he was passing a great estate where roses grew in the hedge, he thought a rose would please her.

No sooner had he plucked it than a monstrous creature — half man, half beast — grabbed him by the throat, saying,
"How dare you steal from me?!"
"But it's just for my little girl!" pleaded the merchant.
"You will bring your daughter here to me, or I shall kill you,"
said the Beast.

When the merchant returned home, he told the story to his family.
Bellinda's heart was moved by her father's sadness. "Let me go to the Beast, father. It's better that I go there than that you should die."
Despite his protests, Bellinda made her way to the Beast's castle.
Very frightened indeed, she arrived at what looked like an empty castle.

Despite this, her every need was provided for: invisible servants brought her food and invisible maids helped her to dress and undress. When darkness fell, the Beast came and sat at the dinner table. Despite the Beast's bad temper and his fearsome appearance, the longer she stayed the more fond Bellinda became of him.

After a few months, Bellinda begged to go home on a visit. The Beast agreed, but gave her a magic ring in which she could see his image: this was to remind Bellinda of her promise to return to him. However, Bellinda stayed away for so long that the Beast began to die without her. It wasn't until she looked into the ring and saw that the Beast's image was fading that she remembered her promise and was very sorry.

Rushing to his side, Bellinda found the Beast on the point of death. She stroked his paw, told him that she loved him very much and then kissed him. This kiss ended the enchantment, for he was really a handsome prince who had offended a sorceress called Superbia. And so Prince Rolando and Bellinda were married with great joy!

When Cinderella wanted to go to the ball, she had nothing to wear, no transport and no servants to wait upon her. Her Fairy Godmother waved her wand to transform a pumpkin into a coach, six mice into horses, a rat into a coachman and six lizards into footmen. Like guardian angels, Fairy Godmothers are there to look after you.

HOW TO CONTACT YOUR FAIRY GODMOTHER

If you want to contact your own Fairy Godmother, you should wish with all your heart for the wisdom of the Fairy Queen. Every night before you sleep, place your hands over your heart and say:

Queen of the Land, Queen of the Sea,
Please send my Fairy Godmother to me!

Something magical will begin to happen that week. Maybe just one leaf on a whole tree will tremble when there is no wind, or you might hear chiming when there are no bells; if this happens your Fairy Godmother is near. Tell her about what's happened or ask for her help, then sit quietly while she speaks inside you. You can safely tell your deepest secrets to your Fairy Godmother. Even when you can't find the words, she will always read your heart.

Fairy Godmother Hotline

Call: 555 016 983 28930056

DAY OR NIGHT   ANY EMERGENCY

Precious Princess

Issue 653

From Sour to Sweet...

Gertrude and Ermintrude, stepsisters of celebrity princess Cinderella, welcomed our reporter to their charming sweet shop, The Candy Box. The sisters first came to the world's attention when their behaviour nearly prevented Cinderella from marrying Prince Charming.

Ermintrude, whose girth has expanded somewhat since becoming a sweet-shop owner, and her sister, Gertrude, charming with rosy cheeks and a spotted pinafore, explained, "We are not really ugly you know, although the way we behaved wasn't very pretty."

Ermintrude sadly explained that after their father died they could not afford a servant and they saw

Gertrude (left) and Ermintrude in their wicked days – it's all behind them now.

> ## "We thought the glass slipper was ours, so we locked Cinders up."

Cinderella as their chance to avoid disagreeable tasks.

"We treated Cinders badly, but all we wanted was to be loved by a man who was wor-thy of our many charms. We made ourselves beautiful for Prince Charming too, but he didn't even look at us."

Nor would their feet fit the tiny slipper that the prince's men brought round the week after the ball. They admit that they kept Cinderella in the attic in an attempt to pre-vent her from being discov-ered as the owner of the lost glass slipper. "But that's all behind us now," they said.

Due to the kindness of Cinderella, both sisters

attended the School for Wayward Princesses, where they became reformed characters. Never quite able to make the grade as princesses, their sweet shop has been a great

"Life has never been so sweet, we're happier than ever."

success. The Candy Box has become the tuck shop for the School for Wayward Princesses, where the girls can come every Wednesday. Some of Cinderella's kindness seems to have rubbed off on her stepsisters – they give a free bag of sweets to all new girls at the school, to make them feel welcome.

While it may be a long way from the palace, royal watchers state that Crown Prince Merrick and his younger brother Admiral Prince Eric of Friseland are both frequent visitors to the shop. Do we hear the chime of wedding bells? Watch this space!

A roaring success: the two sisters hold a plate of their famous fairy cakes.

GOING TO THE BALL

The ball is the place to show off your beauty, elegance and deportment, as well as your lovely jewels and ballgown. If you're still hoping to meet your ideal prince, you may well find him here! Here are a few things to help you get ready for the all-important ball.

PREPARING FOR THE BALL

- Take dance lessons and learn some steps.

- Practise dancing in a long skirt to your own music at home.

- Try eating ice cream elegantly and drinking from a glass while wearing gloves.

The Twelve Dancing Princesses

There were once 12 princesses who, although they were locked in their bedroom every night, had slippers full of holes by the morning. The mystified king announced that the man who was able to discover the cause of this could marry one of the princesses.

Michael, the gardener's boy, called upon the magic cherry tree for help. It showed him how to become invisible by putting a piece of cherry blossom in his coat. He hid in the princesses' wardrobe that night and at midnight the princesses arose, dressed in their ball gowns and dancing slippers and went down a trap door leading to a lake.

On the lake were 12 fairy princes who rowed them over to a dance. Michael hid in a boat and saw how they danced all night. When they returned the next morning, their slippers were full of holes. They had such fun that Michael decided to try dancing himself!

He went to the cherry tree and asked to be dressed like a prince. Then he went to the king and asked for permission to solve the mystery of the slippers. The king agreed and when the princesses next slipped out of the bedroom through the trap door, Michael was already waiting on the other side of the lake to dance with them all.

The princesses thought he danced very well, but the smallest princess liked him best of all. The next morning, Michael went to the king and explained how the slippers came to be worn out.

The king was delighted. He gave Michael a chest full of treasure and asked, "Which princess do you wish to marry?" "Princess Maria," said Michael. And the smallest princess clapped her hands with joy, for she had found the best dancer of all.

DANCE ETIQUETTE

At the ball you can't dance with just anyone you like. It is polite to dance with a selection of guests; that means older partners, officials and other young men, not just your prince! Curtsy to your partner before and after the dance, and don't forget to thank him, even if he stood on your toes! I recommend that you rest after every few dances or you'll become very hot and unprincess-like. Your partner can bring you a refreshing cordial or an ice cream while you sit on the terrace and look at the moon. Your dance card will list the dances that the orchestra will play. Here's an old one of mine – as you'll see I've scribbled a few names on it!

PRINCESS PETAL'S DANCE CARD

Opening Waltz: *King of Olveria*

Military Quick Step: *Colonel Joyson*

Quadrille: *Ambassador Gray*

Gavotte: *Sir Elemire Martin*

Mazurka: *Ensign Paul Scheffer*

Polonaise: *Count Maximilian*

Last Waltz: *Prince Pallas*

HOST YOUR OWN BALL

It's time to have your own princess party! Make invitations like the one shown here to ask your friends to this special occasion. Request that everyone comes wearing a lovely party dress and brings one small gift to put in a sack when they arrive. A prize crown can be awarded to the best-dressed princess, and at the end of the party everyone can take turns to pull a present out of the sack and keep it. Ask your parents to help you make up a bag of little treats, sweets and prizes to award to the winners of the party games.

Invitation

Princess_____ *your name* _____ requests the

company of_____ *your guest* _____

for a Princess Party

on_____ *date* _____at_____ *time* _____

address_____ *your address* _____

Tiaras and pretty dresses will be worn. Please bring a small wrapped gift and one nice treat to eat or drink.

Prizes for the best-dressed princess to be judged

by Queen_____ *your mother's name* _____

PARTY GAMES

Fairy Godmother's Token

All the princesses stand in a ring, with one girl in the middle. Behind their backs, the princesses pass a token (a nut or coin) to each other. The girl in the middle then has to guess where the token is. When she guesses correctly, the princess holding the token goes into the middle.

Princess Photo Statues

Everyone stands up and moves around but when the music stops, all the princesses must stop moving to have their photo taken. Anyone who moves or wobbles is out. Continue playing until there is only one princess left.

Perfect Curtsy

Each princess must take a turn to curtsy with a book balanced on her head. The princesses who manage not to drop the book can take something from the prize bag.

Pop The Witch's Spells

This is a noisy game to be played outside in the garden. First of all blow up some balloons of two different colours, say red and blue, until they are about to pop. Put the red balloons in one bag and the blue balloons in another bag at the end of the garden. These balloons represent spells that have been cast by a wicked witch and the princesses have to pop the balloons by sitting on them. Divide your guests into two teams. When the whistle blows, one princess from each team runs to her team's bag, takes out one balloon, and tries to pop it by sitting on it. When she is successful, she runs back to the team and another princess does the same, until all the balloons are popped. The team that pops all the witch's spells first is the winner.

HAPPILY EVER AFTER

Some princesses are born into the role, and others marry a prince to become one. Whatever type you are, there is one day you will never forget and that's your wedding day!

His Majesty, the King of Olveria, requests the company of

_____

at the wedding of his son, HRH Crown Prince Pallas to Her Serene Highness Princess Petal of Mittelberg

On 21 June, Midsummer's Day

Exchange of Vows in the Chapel of Castle Orcadia 10am
Wedding Breakfast 12.30pm
Festivities and Entertainments 2.30pm
Grand Ball and Buffet 7.30pm
Carriages at Midnight

RSVP
The Royal Chamberlain Moresco
Steward's Office
Castle Orcadia
Olveria

Everyone enjoyed dancing
for hours at our wedding

There was archery
on the lawn for our
wedding guests

Our golden carriage whisked
us away at midnight!

WEDDING BELLS

My lovely friends, Lady Janet and Lady Charlotte
helped me plan my wedding day. I drew a picture of the
kind of dress I wanted and we chose some lovely fabric.
It took many days to sew it all, especially the long train
that my bridesmaids carried. My Fairy Godmother gave
it a special sparkle with her wand!

Guests arrived from far and wide. I was very nervous
about being stared at by so many people, but when I
walked up the aisle and saw my dear prince standing at
the altar, I felt calm.

When we came out on the steps, the guests threw
rose-petals and cheered as the great bells rang.
We had a wonderful day of celebration. After the
wedding breakfast, we had archery on the lawn while we
opened our many gifts. Then, we danced the night away
at a grand ball.

At dawn Prince Pallas and I jumped into our carriage
and drove to the mountains, where we spent
our honeymoon.

On your big day I hope you will
have all you ever dreamed of!

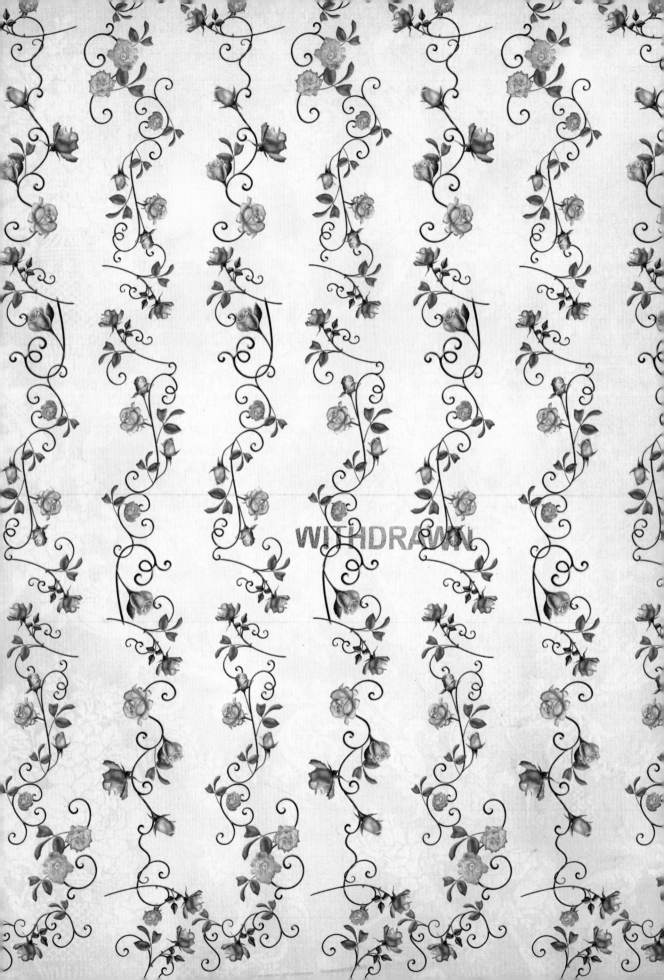